# STINGERS

# Stingers

## Graham Downs

Published by Graham Downs

10 January 2020

Published 10 January 2020 by Graham Downs [Second Edition]

First edition published Published 18 June 2014 by Graham Downs, at http://www.lulu.com/

First Printing: 16 December 2013, in the anthology *I am not Frazzle! And Other Stories for Grown-ups* by Darren Worrow et. al. (ISBN 978-1-291-63765-6)

ISBN 978-0-620-86629-3 (Paperback Edition)

Cover by Melissa Williams Design


http://www.grahamdowns.co.za/

# Dedication

To my darling Elmari,

Thank you for all the love and support. I could not do this without you.

Love always.

## Table of Contents

## One

"All right, you lot. Let's play stingers!"

Little James' heart sank. He hated that game, and all the other kids seemed to hate him. He was a good shot with the tennis ball, but he was terrible at getting out of its way. Besides the other kids, even Mr Evans seemed to have it in for him; he wished he knew why.

James wasn't a huge fan of any sporting activity, now that he came to think of it. He was much happier with his head buried in a book than out here on the field.

He looked around him, at the other kids standing in a circle on the football pitch, all rubbing their hands in anticipation. Then he looked at the school building, no less than a hundred paces away. He wondered if he could run there and sit in the library. Surely Mr Wilson, the English teacher, would protect him.

A sharp pain shot through his right arm, yanking his head out of the clouds. Rubbing his arm, he looked around to see everyone, Mr Evans included, giggling hysterically and pointing at him. Tears welled up in James' eyes, but that only seemed to encourage the pointers.

"Clarke, you're it!" Mr Evans managed through his laughter. "Run, everybody!"

Still rubbing his arm, James walked over to where the ball had rolled.

*May as well make the most of this.*

He picked up the ball and lobbed it towards two of the kids as they ran away. The ball hit Harry on his massive right calf. Harry was a big kid, the same age as James, but easily three times his size. He was the school bully, and there wasn't a student at the school who didn't wish they could one day get the better of him.

The ball sailed through the air gracefully, and didn't hit particularly hard, nor did it roll very far. Harry turned around, scooped the ball up off the ground, and flung it back at James.

"That hurt, you little shit!"

The ball slammed into James' chest, knocking the wind out of him and causing him to fall onto the ground and curl into a little ball himself. As he lay there, sobbing in between deep gulps for air, he sucked dirt and loose grass into his mouth. The rest of the phys. ed. class formed a circle and danced around him, chanting "Poor wittle Clarkey-warkey! Poor wittle Clarkey-warkey!"

Mr Evans was laughing so hard, tears were streaming down his face. Through his laughter, he managed, "Come on, Clarke! Don't be a wuss! Sting them back!"

## Two

Jack Evans sat at their antique dining room table, salivating as his wife Emily approached, carrying a plate full of steaming mashed potatoes and pork sausage. Laying the plate down in front of him, she asked, "How was your day, dear?"

"It was okay, love," replied Jack as he stuck his fork into his sausage. "I had Grade 8-B for phys. ed. today. I've told you about that little runt, James Clarke?"

Mrs Evans nodded as she gingerly sliced a piece off her own sausage. "Oh, Jack, I wish you wouldn't be so mean!"

"The boy's hopeless, I tell you!" exclaimed her husband. "The group played stingers, but he was so scared. Harry Taylor hit him in the chest with the ball, and he went down like a ton of bricks. All he could do was cry. It was hilarious, but it's also disgusting!"

"My love," answered his wife, "he's just a boy. How old is he? Twelve?"

"Thirteen." snapped Jack, "and when I was his age I was walking barefoot to school in the snow!" His wife rolled her eyes and sighed, as Jack continued, "He's so scrawny you can see his collarbones sticking out! That ridiculous phys. ed. tank top he wears is miles too big for him! He needs some muscles on him."

"But, dear. Belittling the boy is not the way to...."

"Nonsense!" he cut off his wife. "A little humiliation is good for anyone! Why, when I was in the army, they made us to do a hundred push-ups in front of our entire squad!"

When Jack Evans got excited, the veins on his massive biceps stuck out under his short white tee-shirt, and the whistle he always wore around his neck bobbed up and down. His wife gave him a reproachful look as it sank into his mashed potatoes.

"I wish you wouldn't wear that to the dinner table, dear."

He gave a blush as he plucked it out and sucked on it.

"Yes, dear," he mumbled. "Wow, this food is fantastic! Did I ever tell you what a wonderful cook you are?"

She just smiled at him. "Oh, Jack. You're incorrigible sometimes!"

He looked at his wife. She was as beautiful as the day he'd first met her, but she didn't understand. As a saleswoman at the stationery shop downtown, she didn't understand what it was like, trying to turn these boys into men. She didn't have what it took to watch them cry, and just laugh at them, knowing that that was how they grew backbones. And she never would.

## Three

James was racing down the short passage from the bathroom to his bedroom, wearing only his towel. He had bathed as quickly as he could, in case his mother had come into their house's only bathroom to use the toilet. The last thing he wanted was for her to see the bruises on his arm and chest, and make a fuss.

He made it about halfway before she walked down the passage. Immediately she stopped and shrieked. "James, what on earth happened to you?!"

James was mortified. He quickly folded his arms over his chest and tried to cover the bruise on his right arm with his left. "N-nothing, Mom," he stammered, "just kids' stuff."

"Nonsense!" exclaimed his mother as she raced towards him and pulled his arms away, exposing his chest. The motion was so fast that James' towel came loose, and he had to grab it with both hands to keep it from falling off. "That's not nothing! That looks like you might have cracked a rib!"

She gently rubbed his sternum, and he winced with pain. When she'd satisfied herself there was nothing broken, she crouched down and cradled his face in her hands. "Come now, tell Mommy what happened." she cooed.

At the tone of her voice, James broke down and cried. He felt humiliated that he hadn't been able to keep from crying in front of his mother, but that only made him cry more.

"Oh, Mommy," he blubbered, "we played Stingers today in phys. ed. Mr Evans threw the ball into my arm, then Harry threw it into my chest, and... and... he called me a wuss, *and they all laughed at me!*"

His mother held her son tightly and pressed his face into her shoulder. He sobbed until the tears stopped.

She took him by the arm and marched him into the kitchen, still wearing nothing but his bath towel. After sitting him down on a chair at the kitchen table, she opened the freezer and threw ice cubes into a dishcloth. She knelt in front of him and gently pressed the makeshift ice-pack onto his chest to stop the swelling.

"Your poor thing," she said sweetly. "My poor, poor baby. Doesn't this teacher know that you're not strong enough for all that rough-housing? And encouraging the other children that way, how irresponsible."

James sniffed away the last of his tears and rubbed his eyes with his fists.

"No, I tell you it's not acceptable," continued his mother. "Tomorrow morning, I'm calling your school!"

James felt his heart skip a beat. His eyes opened like big saucers. Staring at his mother, he pleaded with her. "No, Mommy, no! You'll only make it worse! Please don't do that! It's really not so bad. It'll get better, I promise. You'll see!"

"Nonsense, my love," replied his mother calmly. "I'm calling your school tomorrow and that's that. Now come, let's get you into your PJs and into bed."

She dragged James off to bed, and would not listen to another word.

## Four

"Sir, I'm done!"

Ted Wilson looked up from his marking. Little Olivia had her arm stuck high into the air, with a big satisfied grin on her face. The other kids still had their heads bent down over their worksheets, but Olivia, sitting in the front row, always had to be the over-achiever. Ted sighed.

"No, Olivia, you are not 'done'. You 'have finished with your work'."

Olivia's smile faded for an instant, then re-appeared. "Yes, sir," she said, "I have finished with my work."

"Very well, Olivia," said Mr Wilson, "bring it to me."

The rest of the class glanced up at her, snickering. Someone commented, "Nerd!" Little James Clarke, in the third row, didn't look up, though. He kept his head down, with his eyes firmly fixed on his worksheet.

Olivia walked up to Mr Wilson's desk, clutching her completed work proudly against her chest, lest other kids saw her answers and copied them. She handed the sheet of paper to him and he glanced over it. He nodded. "Very good, Olivia. Wait there a minute, please. I have a favour I need to ask you."

He reached over and grabbed a scrap of notepaper on his desk, then scrawled down a message for Miss Cox, the headmistress. The message explained why he couldn't stay after school to coach cricket that day. Olivia craned to read the message, and Ted eyed her reproachfully. Handing her the note, he said, "Olivia, will you please run down to the office and give this letter to Miss Brown at reception? Ask her to give it to Miss Cox."

"Yes, sir!" said Olivia excitedly, giving a mock salute. She half snatched it from Mr Wilson's hand and turned to run out of the door.

"Oh, and Olivia," said Ted, so she turned around in mid-stride, "Don't go reading it on the way."

Olivia smiled and nodded, then ran out the door excitedly.

After she'd left, the other kids' heads went back down over their work. They were all working furiously, except James. He was staring intently at the paper on his desk, but it was obvious he wasn't registering anything written there; he was just trying not to be noticed. Ted watched James and sighed.

The boy had had a hard year. His father had died just before Christmas, and Ted saw that that still affected him badly. He knew how the other boys picked on James and called him names. Sometimes he stood there and took it, other times he cried and ran away. Not once did he fight back. Ted wished for James' sake that he *would* fight back one day. Just once, to show them he wasn't just a push-over.

Just then, Olivia returned from delivering her message. Before sitting back down, she looked at James and squealed, "James! Your mother's in the office!"

As James looked up, Mr Wilson saw Harry Taylor out of the corner of his eye, blowing a spit-ball into the back of James' neck. James slapped his hand into his neck at the sting and groaned.

"Taylor!" Mr Wilson snapped. "Go see Miss Cox and tell her what you just did!"

Harry got up and strode out of the classroom, an arrogant smile fixed on James.

## Five

Sitting together on their old, furry couch, Harry and his father were the spitting image of each other. There was wrestling on the antique television and a box of Hawaiian pizza on the coffee table in front of them. Harry's plate from the previous week sat on the table beside it, flies buzzing around the mouldy left-overs. Neither the food nor the plate seemed to bother Harry or his father.

Bill Taylor scratched his crotch before reaching forward to take a large slice of pizza out of the box. Wrestling had just cut to a commercial break.

"So son, how did it go at school today?"

"Fine, Dad," replied his son.

"That's good. Did that little Clarke kid give you any more trouble today?"

"No, not since yesterday. He threw a tennis ball at me, but I got him back good! Even made him cry."

His father gave a loud belch, and both he and his son snorted. "Good man!" he said. "Stupid little shits like that need to be taught a lesson."

"Ja," laughed Harry. "His mom was at the school today. Dunno why. Then I got him in the back of the neck with a spit-ball."

"Ja, that's good." muttered his father, holding his arm over his son's chest to quiet him as the commercial break ended. Harry leaned forward to grab another slice of pizza.

Father and son both wore old, faded jeans and tee shirts that seemed too small for them. Bill Taylor's paunch protruded far out from under his shirt, with his son's belly not far behind. Bill took a draught of beer, burped again, and smacked his stomach. His son laughed hysterically.

Suddenly, Bill leapt to his feet and cheered. The Macho Striker had just pinned Sweet Slate to the mat for a three-count. Harry threw his pizza back in the box in disgust. He had been rooting for Sweet Slate.

"Oh, man!" he exclaimed in disappointment.

His father pointed at him and laughed, "Yee-haah! Take that, you loser!

"I don't know how you expected that scrawny Slate to take out Macho, boy. Look at him. He couldn't hurt a fly! Now pay up!"

"Yes dad," sighed Harry as he pulled a note out of his jeans pocket and handed it to his father. Bill took the money from his son without hesitation.

As the ending credits rolled, Bill spoke to his son in a lecturing tone of voice. "Son, *you* are the Macho Striker to that Clarke kid's Sweet Slate. People like us are better than little pipsqueaks like them. Survival of the strongest, you hear? Never let anyone get the better of you, boy."

## Six

Walking home from school that day, James' heart felt like a lump of lead. He walked with his eyes planted firmly on the ground.

*Mom said something to Miss Cox about the bruises. I just know it!*

He was furious with his mother for breaking his trust like that, after he had begged her not to, but even more, he was afraid. He would be the laughingstock of the school now, and the bullying would only get worse.

*This is all I need! I wish Dad were here.*

Mr Clarke had been the rock on which he and his mother depended for as long as James could remember. He remembered afternoons when he walked out of the schoolyard to see the shiny black BMW parked on the street, his father standing on the curb against it, watching for him to appear. He'd always wrapped his arms around James and held him tight with a "How was your day, m'boy?"

All the other kids would walk past him and wave, shouting, "Hi, Mr Clarke!"

He felt so proud in those days, but after his dad died, his mom had to sell that car and buy a second-hand Ford. She had to get a job as a legal secretary. And she was lucky to get it because the partners felt sorry for her after the sudden heart-attack of her husband. He had been a lawyer there, well liked by everyone he met.

Now his mother worked long hours, and they seldom had home cooking anymore. He knew how much she loved him, but....

James looked up with a start at the sound of screeching brakes and a car hooting. A man was leaning out of a car window, shaking his fist. "Watch where you're going, you stupid kid!"

James blushed as he realised that he was standing in the middle of an intersection, and the robot was red. He waved an apology at the man as the car drove past, missing him by a small margin. He hurried to get back onto the pavement, then groaned at the sound of another car hooter.

*Oh, geez, what now?*

He looked over at the shiny silver Audi pulled up next to him. The back window opened, and Olivia stuck her head out. "Hey James, want a lift?"

James smiled. He knew Olivia liked him, but he didn't understand why, and he wasn't interested in girls, anyway. Still, some company would be good. He smiled and nodded. Olivia pushed open the back door and shifted over in the seat to give him space. "Hop in!"

James got in the car and closed the door. He looked in the rear-view mirror to see Olivia's mother put her hand up in greeting. "Hello, James."

"Hi, Mrs Johnson!" replied James, and the car pulled off.

Eighties music was blaring out of the car speakers, and Mrs Johnson was drumming her hands on the steering wheel, to the beat. Olivia grinned at James. "Mom loves this stuff," she said, "but I don't understand it. So, why do you think your mom was at school today?"

"I don't know," James lied. He had a feeling that the whole school would know anyway, soon enough.

He resolved not to talk to his mother that night. If he did, he decided, it would just end up in a fight. His day was fine. That was all she needed to know.

The car continued on its way to his house, with Olivia jabbering in the seat next to him, but he didn't hear any of it. He didn't say another word for the rest of the ride home.

## Seven

As usual, the school hall was buzzing as everyone sat waiting for the teachers to arrive, led by Miss Cox to give the assembly. James sat with the rest of the Grade Eights, on the floor in the front of the hall. The Grade Nines through Grade Tens sat on plastic chairs behind him, and the Grade Elevens and Twelves sat on pews, upstairs in the gallery. The further back you sat in the hall, the more noise there was, and the less chance there was of any student paying attention.

The large double-doors at the back of the hall swung open, and a hush fell over the congregation of students. There was silence except for the scraping of chairs as the children downstairs all stood up when the staff filed in (nobody really cared what those in the gallery did).

When all the teachers had taken their seats on the stage, Miss Cox stepped up to the podium and gave the instruction to be seated. There was more scraping of chairs as the students took their seats; James sat down on the floor with the rest of the Grade Eights.

Miss Cox was a short woman with glasses resting on the bottom of her nose and blonde hair on her head, showing flecks of grey. She began the assembly with a report back on how the previous day's cricket had gone. Mr Wilson hadn't been able to coach them, and so Mr Evans stepped in. Mr Wilson would not be at school today either; he had taken ill, and so his classes for the day would be expected to sit in the hall and study during their periods.

James grimaced in disappointment, but didn't say a word. Being in the front of the hall, the Grade Eights were in Miss Cox's line of sight, and she wasn't known for her leniency.

He liked Mr Wilson, and he always looked forward to his English periods. Mr Wilson was nice to him, and although he never said it, he seemed to understand what James was going through. He also didn't tolerate bullying in his class.

Then, the worst thing that could happen, as far as James was concerned, did. "Now, listen up!" said Miss Cox. "This is important. Little James Clarke," she pointed directly at James. He was horrified! All the Grade Eights turned to look at him, and the children in their chairs craned their heads in his direction. Even some seniors in the gallery half-stood up to get a look at him.

"Little James Clarke," continued Miss Cox, "has been the victim of bullying lately. He hurt his chest badly in Mr Evans physical education class two days ago, and a few of you children laughed at him."

She continued, emphasising each word, "I will not tolerate bullying at our school!

"Because of his poor constitution, I have requested of Mr Evans that he excludes young Mr Clarke from all physical activity from now on."

"And son," she looked at him with what was meant to be a comforting smile on her face, but which to James just looked mocking. "If anybody gives you any trouble, you come straight to me." Looking at the assembly at large again, she repeated, "I will not tolerate bullying at this school!"

James wished the ground would swallow him up. The students got to their feet again for the teachers to leave. Once they had passed, Harry Taylor walked up to him and punched him hard in the shoulder. When James looked at him, he drew his finger across his neck and mouthed "You're dead, Clarkey-warkey."

*I knew it. I just knew it! This will only get worse. I'm done for, now!*

# Eight

That morning, James had his English period just before first break, but he and the rest of the class were in the school hall. Chairs had been rearranged, and desks had been brought in and pushed together.

He was supposed to be studying, but he was doodling on a piece of paper, a little stick figure hanging in a gallows. He imagined the figure to be himself.

When the bell rang for break, the hall emptied quickly. Olivia stood at the door on her way out, looking back at James when she saw he was still sitting at the table.

"Come on, James! Come play!" she squealed.

"No thank you, Olivia," James answered. "I'm not finished yet. I think I'll try to get a little more work done."

"Your loss," shrugged Olivia, and she ran outside. He could hear her squealing and giggling as she joined her friends.

James' bladder had been getting fuller and fuller for the past hour, but he tried desperately to ignore it. He didn't want to think about what could be waiting for him out there. Out there was a hostile wilderness to him, especially after what happened in assembly that morning.

Squeezing his legs together, he tried to focus on his doodles, but the pressure kept building. At last, he gave up.

*What am I doing? I can't live my life in fear! When you got to go, you got to go!*

Slowly, he got up and hobbled to the door leading out into the quad. He stuck his head out and looked around. Boys and girls were standing in clusters, laughing and chatting, and giggling. Nobody seemed to notice him, and there didn't seem to be any sign of Harry Taylor. He knew that he had to avoid Harry in particular, especially after what happened in assembly.

He looked across at the door to the bathroom. It was a

short distance from the hall, but he would have to cross through the mass of children. To him, it felt like a mile away.

Walking quickly (but he hoped inconspicuously) he made his way across the quad. He stopped and listened at the bathroom door, but he would not have been able to hear anything in there, with the noise outside. He cautiously pulled the door open and listened. There didn't seem to be anyone inside. Breathing a sigh of relief, he opened the door and entered, closing it behind him.

Out of the three stalls in the bathroom, one door was locked, and there was no-one at the urinals. This encouraged James; he figured if he was just quick about it, he could finish before anyone else arrived. He wasn't about to stand at a urinal, though, out in the open with his back to the room.

He pushed open the door next to the occupied stall and walked in. Pushing the door closed behind him, he lifted the toilet seat and stood in front of it, unzipping his trousers.

*Ah, relief! This isn't so bad! What was I so afraid of?*

About halfway through, he heard a door creaking behind him. He'd forgotten to lock the stall door! Glancing over his shoulder, he saw Harry Taylor's face, grinning evilly at him.

Before he could react, Harry grabbed him with one hand on the back of his shirt collar, and another on his belt. He yanked James backwards in mid-stream, causing him to spray all over the outside of the toilet bowl, the wall behind it, and the floor.

"Now listen here, you little shit!" hissed Harry, as he forced James' head down into the bowl. "You've caused crap for me for the last time!"

Harry flushed the toilet, and as James spluttered and gasped for air, inhaling toilet water, Harry laughed.

When the toilet wouldn't flush anymore, and James' bladder was empty, Harry picked him up and pressed him into a seated position over the open toilet bowl. Harry punched him repeatedly in the face, yelling furiously at him about how he was not be made a fool of, and that stupid little runts like James should know their place. Blood and tears blinded James' eyes, mixing with the toilet water which ran down his face. When he'd finished, Harry stepped back, took a deep breath, and reached into his pocket. He produced a flick-knife and pushed a button on the hilt, releasing the blade. James eyes went wide as he saw the knife, and saw Harry's eyes glancing at his still-open fly, and what was still dangling out of it.

James' hands went immediately to his crotch, and he screamed, "No! Help me, please help me! Not there, please not there!"

Harry let out a low, sick laugh. "You stupid little git! I wouldn't touch you *there* with a six-foot pole! Now, it's time to teach you a lesson."

It seemed to happen in slow motion. Harry pulled his arm back, and plunged the knife into James' stomach. James felt a weird sort of pain, a distant pain, as though in a dream. Harry removed the blade, and blood gushed out of the wound. James' complexion went snow white. He felt like he was going to throw up. He hardly felt the second wound in his stomach, and by the third, he was no longer aware of anything but the sensation of blood oozing out of his body.

## Nine

Harry came storming into the lounge to find his father sitting on the couch, belly sticking out, watching infomercials and drinking a beer.

Bill Taylor gawked at his son, heaving for air. The front of Harry's shirt was drenched in blood, and he held the flick-knife at his side, the blade still out, dried blood caked on the point.

"What the hell happened to you? Is that your blood?" demanded his father.

"No, Dad," gasped Harry, a sick smile forming across his face. "I taught that Clarke pipsqueak a lesson, just like you said!"

Bill got up from his chair so fast he knocked his beer can off the coffee table. It landed sideways on the old dusty carpet, causing beer to spill out and soaking into it. In a flash, he was standing in front of Harry, gripping his arms like a vice, shaking him. Harry had such a fright he dropped the knife. It landed on its point into the carpet, narrowly missing the boy's foot.

"Shit, boy! What did you do?"

"I... found him in the toilet," stammered Harry, now more out of the shock of being grabbed by his father than his breathlessness from the run home from school. "I gave him a bog-wash, and then I stabbed him." His smile returned somewhat as he described the scene to his father. "I felt good, Dad. It felt great to put someone in their place." He looked up at Bill, with eyes like saucers. "Aren't you proud of me?"

Bill released his vice-grip on his son and stepped back. For a moment, Harry thought it would all be okay, that he'd finally made his father proud. He relaxed, and as he did, Bill pulled his arm back and smashed his fist into Harry's nose. Harry went down, clutching his nose, blood streaming down his face and soaking into his shirt, mixing with the now-dried blood of James Clarke.

His father kicked him hard in the ribs where he lay. "You stupid shit!" he exclaimed. "You good-for-nothing son of a bitch! What the hell are we going to do now? The cops will be all over us in a minute."

Tears streamed down Harry's face, as he sobbed uncontrollably.

"That's right, you worthless baby. Cry!" His father was screaming now, his face was red with rage, and it looked as if his eyes would pop right out of his head. "Get out! I never want to see you again, as long as I live!"

Harry scrambled to his feet, clutching his chest with one hand and his nose with the other. Tears continued to run down his cheeks. He looked at his father for some kind of understanding, but there was nothing but hate in Bill Taylor's eyes. Harry turned on his heels and ran out of the house.

## Ten

Mrs Clarke sat in the small waiting room, just outside the operating room. Her head was buried in her hands, and Mrs Johnson sat beside her with her arms around her shoulders. Olivia sat quietly sobbing in the seat opposite, her hands clasped together on her lap.

"I'm sorry, Mrs Clarke," said Olivia, "I heard the screaming coming from the boys' bathrooms, and then I saw Harry running out. There was so much blood." She buried her own head in her hands as a fresh bout of sobbing ensued.

Olivia had hesitated for a moment before rushing into the bathroom. She knew she shouldn't go in there, but when she heard the screams, something made her go anyway. When she entered the bathroom, she saw blood running across the floor out of an open stall door. Steeling herself to enter, she saw James lying there on his back, and she saw the blood. Olivia screamed and passed out.

"That's all right, Olivia," sobbed James' mother. "You did the right thing. If it weren't for you, my boy might be dead right now. Thank you for what you did."

"Mrs Clarke?"

Ava Clarke looked up to see Dr Patel standing there, still wearing his surgical cap. Blood still stained the front of his scrubs, but she could see that he had tried hastily to clean them before coming to see her. Her son's blood.

"Your son sustained serious injuries, ma'am," the doctor explained. "He was stabbed five times in his abdomen, and he lost a lot of blood."

Ava gasped away a sob. Looking up at the doctor, she pleaded, "Will he be okay, doctor? Will my boy be all right?"

"We have repaired the perforation to his stomach as best we could," replied the doctor, "but your son lost a lot of blood.

He's still under anaesthetic, but he's been taken to recovery now. All we can do is wait."

"C-can I see him?" asked James' mother.

"Not as yet, ma'am," replied Dr Patel. "The nurse will call you when he's awake."

Turning to Grace Johnson, Dr Patel pointed with his thumb at the police officer who was standing patiently at the entrance to the waiting room. "Mrs Johnson, that officer would like to talk to your daughter now, about what she saw."

Mrs Johnson looked over at her daughter. "Are you up to it, love?" she asked.

Olivia took a deep breath and looked her mother in the eyes. "Yes, Mom," she said bravely. "I need to. I don't want Harry to get away."

## Eleven

"Nothing like this has ever happened at our school before," Miss Cox said in a sombre voice, looking around at the teachers congregated in the small staff room, "and I've called this emergency staff meeting for two reasons. First, to decide what to do about it, and second, to make sure that nothing like it ever happens again."

"I called the police an hour ago," said Miss Brown. "They have already been to the Taylors' house, but Harry is not there. His father says he hasn't seen him."

"I hear they're watching the house," interjected another teacher. "If he comes back, they'll arrest him."

"Yes," continued the school receptionist, "and they've asked that we notify them immediately if he tries to come back to school."

"I hope for his sake he doesn't," snapped Ted Wilson. "If I see the little shit, I'll kill him. I hate bullies! Kids like that shouldn't be allowed to grow up."

"That's enough of that, Mr Wilson," said Miss Cox. "And there's no need for that kind of language in my staff room either. We will let the police deal with this." She looked around at the assembled staff, "I will not tolerate any kind of vigilantism. Is that clear?"

Mr Evans swallowed hard and said, "Maybe the Clarke kid had it coming to him. Don't take me the wrong way. I really hope he's okay. But maybe this will teach him a little about how to stand up for himself. Weak kids like that either learn to fight back, or they're walked all over, their whole lives."

"How dare you!" growled Mr Wilson as he stood up and lunged towards Jack Evans. "I'll rip your head off!"

Jack sank back into his chair as Ted towered over him, ready to grab him by the neck and squeeze the life out of him.

"Enough!" boomed Miss Cox. A hush fell over the entire staff room; nobody there had ever heard their headmistress use such a tone before. "Fighting amongst ourselves won't get us anywhere. We need a way forward."

"A good way forward is to get this Neanderthal out of my sight, and out of this school," growled Mr Wilson as he took his seat again. "Violence and humiliation never taught a child anything. It never taught me anything when I was his age."

"You're right, Ted. I'm sorry," replied Jack as he suddenly realised who he had been speaking to. "I know what your father did to you. I didn't mean that the kid should be beaten to within an inch of his life or anything. I just meant...."

"I know exactly what you meant," snapped Ted, "and your apology is *not* accepted."

## Twelve

"Hello, young lady. I am Officer Wood." The policeman smiled at Olivia.

He sat in a plush leather chair behind an enormous desk in a generously large office. A filing cabinet rested against the wall beside a gargantuan window, which let the sun stream in warmly. It was Dr Patel's office, which he had lent them for the interview, while he went about seeing to his other patients. The office was warm and inviting, but Grace, sitting next to her daughter opposite Officer Wood, felt the coldness and arrogance of it all under the circumstances.

Olivia looked up at her mother, who nodded and smiled, letting her know that it was all right to speak to the policeman.

"Hello Officer Wood," said Olivia bravely. "I'm Olivia Johnson."

"It's a pleasure to meet you, Miss Johnson," smiled Wood. "What a brave girl you are! Would you tell me what happened today, when you found the young Mr Clarke?"

Olivia swallowed hard, then began to tell the policeman exactly what had happened. Officer Wood smiled warmly, nodding his understanding and handing her tissues when she sobbed. Sometimes she stopped, unable to go on, and Officer Wood waited patiently, asking her if she was ready to continue, telling her to take her time.

When she had finished, her mother was sobbing. She could not believe that her daughter could be so brave. She wrapped her arm around her daughter's shoulders, pulling her close. Kissing Olivia on the head, Grace said through her tears, "I'm so proud of you, my beautiful daughter! I'm so sorry you had to go through that!"

"It's okay, Mom," smiled Olivia. "Please don't cry. I'm okay, I promise." Looking up at the officer, she said, "Officer

Wood, please would you promise me one thing? Please promise me you'll catch Harry?"

Officer Wood smiled at her and, after hesitating for only a moment, replied, "We will do everything we can, young lady. I promise. You were a big help. I don't think we'd be able to catch him if it wasn't for what you told me today."

"Thank you, Officer," said Grace. "Tell me, what will happen when you catch him?"

"If he's found guilty," replied Wood, "he'll be sent to a juvenile detention centre. A judge will then determine whether his father is fit to raise him. I've heard from other sources that they don't have a very stable home life."

"But let's take this one step at a time," continued Officer Wood. "Only time will tell."

## Thirteen

The first thing James saw when he was awake was his mother's face, staring down at him and smiling. He looked around and saw Olivia and her mother sitting on chairs beside his bed. Returning his gaze to his mother, he asked "W-what happened?"

Mrs Clarke broke down in tears. "Oh, my beautiful boy!" she exclaimed. "You were stabbed. But you're okay now. I'm so glad you're okay!"

"Stabbed?" asked James as his mother leant down and hugged him so hard it caused the sharp pain in his stomach to become almost unbearable. "What do you mean?"

"Oh, James!" exclaimed Olivia. "I'm so sorry! I was too late. You almost died!"

James looked at Olivia, then his mother, then at Mrs Johnson, who was wringing her hands together with a worried expression on her face. "What happened?" asked James desperately. "Why am I in the hospital? Why is my stomach so sore? Would someone please tell me what happened?"

It was Grace Johnson who spoke. "You were stabbed, son. By Harry Taylor, in the school toilets. My daughter found you. The doctor said you could've died, if it hadn't been for her."

"Thanks," replied James sheepishly. He looked at Olivia, who blushed. "But I still don't understand."

Slowly, Olivia began relating the story of how she had heard the scream from the bathroom and seen Harry running out. Her voice broke a little as she described the blood, and she broke down completely when she got to the part where she discovered James, blood oozing from his stomach, and water dripping from his hair.

"I thought you were dead!" she sobbed.

Just then, Mr Wilson entered the room. Standing at James' bed, he smiled and said "Hi, James. I'm glad to see you're awake!"

James looked at his English teacher in surprise. "Thanks, Mr Wilson. But, what are you doing here?"

"I wanted to find out how my favourite pupil was doing," replied Mr Wilson, reaching down and ruffling James' hair. "Fourth period English wouldn't be the same without you. Aside from Olivia, nobody understands Hamlet like you do. I may as well be talking to a brick wall, if it weren't for the two of you!"

James laughed, then winced at the pain in his stomach.

"I'm afraid you'll have to do without him for a while, Mr Wilson," said Mrs Clarke softly, smiling at her son. "Dr Patel says it will be at least six weeks before he's well enough to go back to school."

"Oh, don't worry about that," replied Mr Wilson. "Olivia will have to do." Turning back to James, he said, "You just get well soon, son. You'll be back in my class before you know it!"

## Fourteen

Jack Evans was sitting on the couch watching television. His wife was doing stock-take at the stationery shop and would not be home for dinner. Jack had ordered takeaways from the pizza place. As he took a slice out of the box on the coffee table, he heard the doorbell ring. Cursing under his breath, he put the slice back in the box and went to answer it.

It surprised him when he opened the door to see Ted Wilson standing there, wearing a thick bomber jacket and holding a six-pack of beers in his hand.

"Hi, Jack," he said, "is this a bad time?"

"Well, actually...." began Jack.

Ted cut him off. "Glad to hear it! I just wanted to say that I am sorry for how I behaved in the staff meeting today." He held up the beers. "I brought these as a peace offering. May I come in?"

Jack scratched the back of his head and sighed. "I guess so. Come in, Ted."

He led Ted into the lounge and motioned towards the armchair in the corner, next to the television. "Take a seat," he said.

Ted put the beers onto the coffee table and sat down. He pointed to the pizza. "Having dinner?"

"The wife's working late," replied Jack. "I had to sort myself out tonight. Would you like a slice?"

"Don't mind if I do," said Ted, reaching for a slice of the pizza. "Have a beer."

Jack took one. Twisting off the cap, he looked at Ted and nodded at the thick jacket the man was wearing. "You cold, Ted? It's twenty-two today. I'm pretty warm, myself."

"Oh, you know me," replied Ted with a chuckle. "I'm always cold."

"Ja," answered Jack, "that I do. Listen, Ted. I'm sorry for what I said today. I really forgot what happened with you and your father."

"You know," sighed Ted, "my father used to beat me to within an inch of my life every chance he got. It only got worse after my mother died. There was a time I thought I'd never get away from him. I hate to see children being treated like garbage. It's just not right."

"I understand," said Jack as he reached for another slice of pizza. "You never told me how you *did*. Get away from him, I mean."

"Oh, never mind that," replied Ted coolly, wiping the crumbs off his hands. He reached in under his jacket and said, "Just know that I will never let anyone treat another child the way my father treated me."

Jack glanced up at him as he took the slice of pizza out of the box. His eyes went wide, and he dropped it back down immediately. Ted Wilson was holding a pistol pointed squarely at his chest.

## Fifteen

Bill Taylor swerved to avoid someone walking across the road in front of him. As he sped through the red light, he glanced in his rear-view mirror. He only had time to see the man he'd just narrowly missed, shaking his fist.

Harry hadn't come home last night.

*I hope that fool boy didn't go to the cops. We're both done for, then!*

Reaching down, he tuned the radio to his favourite station. He looked ridiculous, whipping his head back and forth to the heavy metal music. He hadn't had long hair in over a decade, but he felt like it was the nineties all over again. Things were so much simpler then. When Harry's mother was still alive. She'd have known what to do.

*Why did she have to leave me? Why did she have to get cancer?*

Bill didn't know where he was going, but he knew that he had to get away. He glanced down at the passenger seat, to the shopping bag he'd just bought at the liquor store. He reached in and pulled out a beer.

*If that stupid son of mine went to the cops, this town's not safe for me.*

Throwing his head back and pouring the contents of the can of beer down his throat, he jerked the steering wheel sharply to the left, onto the on-ramp for the highway. Having downed the beer in one gulp, he threw the empty can out of the driver's window and took out another, as he heard a car hooting in the traffic behind him.

Bill drove for another two hours before seeing the off-ramp for the town where his mother lived. He almost missed it, weaving his car left and right over the highway as he tried to make out the fuzzy letters on the sign.

*Yes! Mother! She'll know what to do.*

He reached into the packet on the passenger seat for another beer, but there were none left.

*Shit! I must get more beer.*

Bill took the off-ramp at breakneck speed, not stopping for the traffic light at the other end. The sounds of more hooting assaulted his ears, and then he heard the screeching of tyres and a crash behind him, but he didn't care.

He didn't stop until he saw the bottle store on the corner. Then, in his drunken stupor, he jerked the wheel to the left, aiming to park on the street.

But he misjudged the distance and sent the car crashing through the front window of the store. People inside screamed as the car smashed through the shelves displaying bottles of hard liquor, sending them all over the floor. The airbag of Bill's car deployed, slamming his head back against the headrest of the driver's seat.

People came rushing up to his car to see if he was all right, but he noticed none of them. His neck had snapped, and his lifeless head bopped grotesquely against the airbag, rocking with the momentum of the impact.

## Sixteen

"James! Olivia's here!" yelled Mrs Clarke after opening the front door.

James came running down the passage from his room. He was clutching his stomach, more out of habit than pain.

"I brought your homework," smiled Olivia as she held out a worksheet. "Mr Wilson says you are to read pages twenty-five to thirty of your textbook. And complete this."

"Thanks Olivia," smiled James as he took the sheet of paper from her. "Let's sit at the kitchen table."

Olivia took her seat and gratefully accepted Mrs Clarke's offer of some lemonade.

"How are you feeling," she asked James, "seven weeks after the stabbing, and one week after your stitches came out?"

"I'm feeling okay," said James. "Just a little scared of going back to school. I don't know how I'll face everybody. Especially Mr Evans."

"Oh, didn't you hear?" asked Olivia. "Nobody's seen Mr Evans since the week of the stabbing. I don't know what happened to him; maybe he got another job or something."

James looked confused, but after a moment a relieved smile touched his face. "Maybe," he nodded. "I'm just glad I don't have to be in his phys. ed. class anymore."

"I thought you might say that," laughed Olivia. "And then there's Harry. Nobody knows where he is, but Mr Wilson said to tell you you won't have to worry about him anymore, either."

James looked surprised. That was not something he thought Mr Wilson would say. "What do you think he meant by that?" he asked Olivia. "I mean, how can he be so sure?"

"I don't know," shrugged Olivia. "But the police have been looking for him ever since the stabbing. I don't think they've caught him yet. Maybe he just means that Harry would never show his face anywhere near the school again. I'm sure they'd arrest him if he did."

"Maybe," agreed James. "Hey, who's the new boy's phys. ed. teacher anyway?"

"His name is Mr Davies," she replied. "And boy is he old! His hair is all white; he must be at least... forty."

"What's he like?"

"I don't know much about him, but the other boys say he's okay. They say they have fun. And I've seen them on the field sometimes during their periods. They're always laughing and running around."

"Well," James said nervously, "I have phys. ed. tomorrow. I hope he doesn't make me exercise."

"He'd better not!" interjected his mother, who had been half-listening to the conversation as she was putting a load of washing into the machine. "Especially after what you've been through. I told them last time that your constitution was too weak for all that rough-housing. I have half a mind to go down to the school tomorrow and—"

"No!" cried James, tears already welling up in his eyes. "Please, Mom, not again! I just want to make a fresh start. I was only joking, anyway. I'm doing fine. Let me fight my own battles, Mom. Please?"

Rolling her eyes, Mrs Clarke sighed as she continued with the washing.

## Seventeen

The next morning in assembly, James felt everyone's eyes on him. Some children looked as though they pitied him, but most just seemed glad to see him. One of the Grade Tens had even offered to let James sit next to him, so he didn't have to sit on the floor. That had really surprised him; none of the seniors had even bothered to talk to him before! He declined, though. He just wanted to be with his friends again.

The children got to their feet as usual, for the teachers to file in, led by Miss Cox. It struck James how familiar everything looked, as if nothing at all had changed. It was strange not to see Mr Evans, though. As Miss Cox took to the podium and instructed everyone to be seated, James caught Mr Wilson's eye. The English teacher was staring directly at him, nodding his head slowly, with a knowing smile on his face. James thought it strange, but he had missed Mr Wilson. Maybe he just felt the same way.

"Before we begin," said Miss Cox, giving James a bit of a fright, "I would like to welcome James Clarke, of Grade 8-B, back to school."

James groaned as Miss Cox continued. *Here we go again!*

"As many of you know, young Mr Clarke was the unfortunate victim of a stabbing on our school premises, seven weeks ago.

"Our school has never experienced such a terrible act before, and I pray we never shall again. The alleged perpetrator, a fellow Grade Eight pupil called Harry Taylor, is being hunted by the police. When they find him," she looked directly at James and added, "and they *will* find him, he will stand trial for his crimes and be punished to the maximum extent of the law."

Miss Cox finished by saying, "In any event, I am extremely pleased to see Mr Clarke back on his feet, as it were, and I hope you will join me in wishing him the speediest recovery, and everything of the best for the rest of his school career."

At once, all the students were on their feet. Joined by the teachers, they gave James a hearty round of applause.

James sighed as he stared at the floor, trying to make himself invisible.

After the applause had died down, and everyone had returned to their seats, Miss Cox's tone changed. "And now," she announced, "on to the business of the day."

*I just want to be left alone, to live my life like a normal kid. Why can't they just leave me alone?*

## Eighteen

James shuffled nervously into the change room next to the gym. The other children were excitedly pulling off their school shirts. Some already had their gym vests on underneath, while others rummaged excitedly through their kit bags to grab theirs, which they pulled on with enthusiasm. Nobody had ever been quite this excited for one of Mr Evans' phys. ed. periods!

Gingerly, James began unbuttoning his shirt and pulling it out of his trousers. He was worried that the others would tease him about his scars. Mostly, though, they paid no notice, except for Timmy Hall, who pointed at them and asked concernedly, "Do they hurt?"

"A little," replied James before looking up to see who had asked. When he saw, it shocked him. Timmy had always been Harry's right-hand man. He said nothing to James unless Harry did first, and then more often than not, it was just to repeat what Taylor had said. James often wondered if Timmy even *had* a mind of his own.

Seeing his reaction, Timmy just smiled at him and patted him encouragingly on the back.

"James," said Timmy solemnly as he pulled on his gym shorts. "I'm sorry for everything I did to you. When Harry and I used to tease you, I thought we were just having fun. After he stabbed you... I can't believe he would ever go so far. Friends?" Timmy stuck out his hand for James to shake.

James was speechless. Slowly, he looked up at Timmy and managed a shy smile, and then gingerly took Timmy's hand.

"Thanks, mate!" said Timmy, shaking James' hand vigorously. "Now let's go play!"

The class herded in, chattering to each other, and the sounds of their voices mingled with the squeaking of bare feet on the smooth, glazed gym floor.

James shuffled along at the back of the class. Nervously, he wrung his hands together as his eyes darted around. He wasn't sure he was ready for this, but at least it was in the gym, not out on the field like last time.

"Settle down, children!" came a voice from the back of the gym. It was loud and authoritative, but somehow also soft and caring, perhaps even a little playful.

James stared at the figure of Mr Davies. He was a tall man. And fit—although maybe not as fit as Mr Evans had been. With his short silver hair and moustache, he stood casually, his arms slightly outstretched, inviting the children to stand in a half-circle around him and enjoy the fun they were about to have together. James was definitely not expecting *any* fun. He was just hoping to survive.

When the children had taken their places around Mr Davies, he announced something that caused James' heart to feel as though it were about to leap out of his chest: "Today, we're playing Stingers!"

The children all cheered, but James groaned loudly as his head fell forward and his eyes stared at the ground. Mr Davies walked up to him and looked at him until James lifted his head and looked back at the teacher.

"You're that Clarke boy, aren't you? The one who Miss Cox was talking about this morning?"

"Y-yes, sir," answered James meekly.

"Well, son, welcome to my class. I'm sorry for what happened to you, and I'm glad you're on the mend. There's nothing like getting back on the horse, though, is there?"

James turned pale. He just wanted to run, to get as far away as possible.

Just then, Timmy piped up. "Sir, I think maybe we should let James sit this one out. His stomach is still sore from the- from what happened to him. Can't he just watch? Just this once?"

46

James glanced towards Timmy and gave a sheepish smile. He still wasn't sure why Timmy was being so nice to him, but he was grateful.

"Nonsense!" was Mr Davies' response. "Everybody plays! Besides, we will be gentle," he met each student's gaze with level eyes, "won't we?"

The students all muttered their assent.

"Excellent. Now, who wants to be in first?"

Gary stuck up his hand. "Me, please, sir."

*Oh, great. Another one of Harry's ex-cronies. This is going to be a long period.*

Mr Davies handed the tennis ball to Gary. "Take your positions!"

Gary walked over and stood on the line, marking the centre of the gym floor. James didn't understand, but Timmy took him by the arm and led him to the wall at the end of the room. They joined the others, who were standing against it.

Mr Davies moved to the side of the court. "On your marks! Get Set! Go!"

As he said "Go", the students all bolted in different directions. James suddenly stood alone, with Gary looking at him and grinning evilly. True to Mr Davies' instructions, though, Gary lobbed the ball under-hand. There would have been ample time for James to get out of the way, but he found that he couldn't move. The ball hit him on the shoulder, bounced off, and rolled away.

James picked up the ball, and Gary ran. When James turned around, he saw Gary and Timmy standing close to each other, and he quickly threw the ball at them. Timmy deftly twisted his body so that the ball hit him on the side of the arm, picked it up, and looked around for a likely target.

"You're out, James!" yelled Mr Davies.

James looked at the teacher incredulously. "What do you mean, sir?"

"That's how we play in this class, son. You get hit, you're in, until you hit someone, then you're out. Better luck next time!"

Sitting on the bench watching the rest of the class continue their game, James smiled. He never knew there was any way of being "out" in Stingers. Mr Evans had just had them play until the period was over, and it wasn't unheard of for him to be hit ten times or more in a single game. This, he could probably handle. In fact, phys. ed. might just be something he could even learn to enjoy.

*Well, I wouldn't go* that *far!*

## Help the Author – Review this Book

Reviews are the lifeblood of an author, especially a self-published one. They help other readers find books that might interest them, and open the door to loads of marketing opportunities.

So if you enjoyed this book, the author would greatly appreciate it if you'd return to the place where you bought it, and write a few words explaining what you thought.

Your review doesn't need to be an essay—although it can be as long as you want it to be. Just a few sentences describing whether you liked it or not are just fine.

If you're really uncomfortable writing anything, you can also simply rate the book (from one to five stars) on social reading site Goodreads, without necessarily writing a review.

If you have the Goodreads app installed on your iOS or Android device, simply use it to scan the barcode on the back cover of this book.

## About the Author

Graham Downs is a South African author of short stories, flash fiction, and novelettes, in a variety of genres. *Memoirs of a Guardian Angel* is his longest work to date.

He currently lives in Alberton, Gauteng, with his wife and their dog, Becky. He spends a good portion of his free time reading and, as with his writing, he reads books in a huge range of genres and lengths. He's also passionate about South African authors—particularly independently published ones.

If you want to keep up with Graham's writing journey, you can sign up for his e-mail newsletter at https://www.grahamdowns.co.za/. You'll get a free book if you do.

**More by Graham Downs**

Look for these books where you found this one, or ask your local store to stock them:

# Fantasy / Paranormal

- *Memoirs of a Guardian Angel*
- *Heaven and Earth: Paranormal Flash Fiction*
- *Billy's Zombie*
- *A Petition to Magic*
- *Tales From Virdura*

# Thriller / Romance

- *Heritage of Deceit*